Tanya and the
Magic Wardrobe

To my Mary – P. G.

For my mother – S. I.

Dance Term Glossary

ballotté (from *ballotter*, to toss): a jump beginning on two legs and ending on one.
jeté (from *jeter*, to throw): a jump forward from one foot to the other;
    it can be big or small.
pas de bourrée (linking step): three tiny steps that link one movement to the next.
pas de chat (step of the cat): a jump with both feet up, then both down.
pirouette (from *pirouetter*, to whirl): a turn around on one foot while the other foot
    is pulled to the opposite knee.
plié (from *plier*, to bend): a bend, with both knees out, heels in.

The ballet story of *Coppélia*, by E. T. A. Hoffmann, has been adapted for this telling.

Text copyright © 1997 by Patricia Lee Gauch. Illustrations copyright © 1997 by Satomi Ichikawa.
All rights reserved. This book, or parts thereof, may not be reproduced in any form without
permission in writing from the publisher, Philomel Books, a division of The Putnam & Grosset Group,
200 Madison Avenue, New York, NY 10016. Philomel Books, Reg. U.S. Pat. & Tm. Off.
Published simultaneously in Canada. Printed in Hong Kong by South China Printing Co. (1988) Ltd.
Book design by Gunta Alexander. The text is set in Horley Old Style.

Library of Congress Cataloging-in-Publication Data
Gauch, Patricia Lee. Tanya and the magic wardrobe / Patricia Lee Gauch; illustrated by Satomi Ichikawa.
p. cm. Summary: When Tanya and her mother arrive early to see a performance of "Coppelia," Tanya
wanders off and meets an old woman who loves dance as much as she does. [1. Ballet dancing — Fiction.]
I. Ichikawa, Satomi. ill. II. Title. PZ7.G2315Tap 1997 [E]—dc20 96-22012 CIP AC
ISBN 0-399-22940-X (hardcover) 10 9 8 7 6 5 4 3 2 1 First Impression

Tanya and the Magic Wardrobe

PATRICIA LEE GAUCH

illustrated by

SATOMI ICHIKAWA

PHILOMEL BOOKS / NEW YORK

The night before Tanya and her mother and her
sister, Elise, were to go to town, Tanya couldn't sleep.
For the first time she would go to the real Ballet. For
the first time she would see dancers dance *Coppélia*,
the ballet about the doll who came to life.

And so the next day Tanya and her mother and her
sister rode a bus and a subway, and walked three long,
wintery blocks.

But when they arrived, the theater was closed.
They'd arrived an hour early by mistake! "Oh, no,"
Mother said out loud.

Tanya was dancing with the *Coppélia* sign to keep
warm, when a woman with programs peeked out of
the gate. "Such winds!" she whispered. "Step inside."
And they did.

Tanya's mother and Elise chatted with the woman with the programs. But the theater was so quiet and dark, the carpet so soft that Tanya began to dance. And when a woman with feathery tutus on her arm bustled down the aisle, Tanya danced right down the aisle after her, *pas de chat, pas de chat.*

"Who's this?" the woman said when she discovered Tanya behind her.

"A dancer," Tanya said, shyly. ". . . I love tutus."

"Ah." The woman smiled. "I am a dancer, too, and I love tutus."

"You?" said Tanya. The woman was very old.

"Me," she said. She glanced at a little clock hanging on a chain around her neck, then hung the tutus on a rack, and went to an old, green wardrobe at the back of the room.

There she opened the lock with
a brass key and took out of the
wardrobe a shimmery pink tutu.

"Sleeping Beauty," she said,
holding the ribbony costume up.
"The prince sees her in this when
he wakes her after a hundred years
of sleep—and they dance."

"Oh," said Tanya.

The old woman did a small
pirouette.

She went back to the green wardrobe,
reached into the other side, and showed
Tanya a brown-weave sack of a costume,
then a silvery one.

"The old beggar woman," *plié, plié,*
"who turned into a fairy godmother,"
jeté, jeté, "and turned Cinderella into
a princess."

Tanya felt like Cinderella. Her feet
started to move, too.

The woman, somehow lighter and lighter of foot
now, grabbed a lavender nightgown. "Clara!" she
said. Tanya knew it was the *Nutcracker Suite's* Clara.
"Clara worries about the poor, wounded nutcracker
captain," *pirouette* and bow, "and fights the dangerous
Mouse King."

Tanya knew the Mouse King! She became him, his
tail twirling, sword in hand, *touché, touché, pas de
bourrée, pas de bourrée.* The two dancers laughed.

Younger and younger now, the woman swept around the room. "And now, once upon a time," she said, touching one costume after another, "there was a doctor who was also a toymaker. Dr. Coppélius." The woman grabbed a top hat and scarf.

"How he loved his puppets and toys," she said as she danced, *ballotté, ballotté.* "But the doctor makes a new doll, the doll he will love best. Beautiful Coppélia!"

She handed ribbons to Tanya, who became the beautiful Coppélia.

"She is the doctor's secret. All he can think of. At the end of each day, he even sits her on his balcony to show her off to the village. If only his Coppélia could come alive!

"The village girls become curious—and jealous—of the pretty, pretty girl always sitting on the doctor's balcony.

"They sneak into his house when he's not there and discover his windup toys: his tin soldiers and mad hatters, his golden cocks, and they wind them up. The toys all come to life—*tickedy, tickedy, tickedy.*

"Then one girl discovers the beautiful Coppélia hidden in a basket!

"But she is only a doll, the village girl discovers, just as Dr. Coppélius unlocks the door. The girls all hide!

"Dr. Coppélius doesn't notice. He has magic potion to make his doll come alive. 'Live, Coppélia!' he says.

"Coppélia is stiff at first, but then, like magic, she dances. They both dance and dance, every dance in the world, and all around the room.

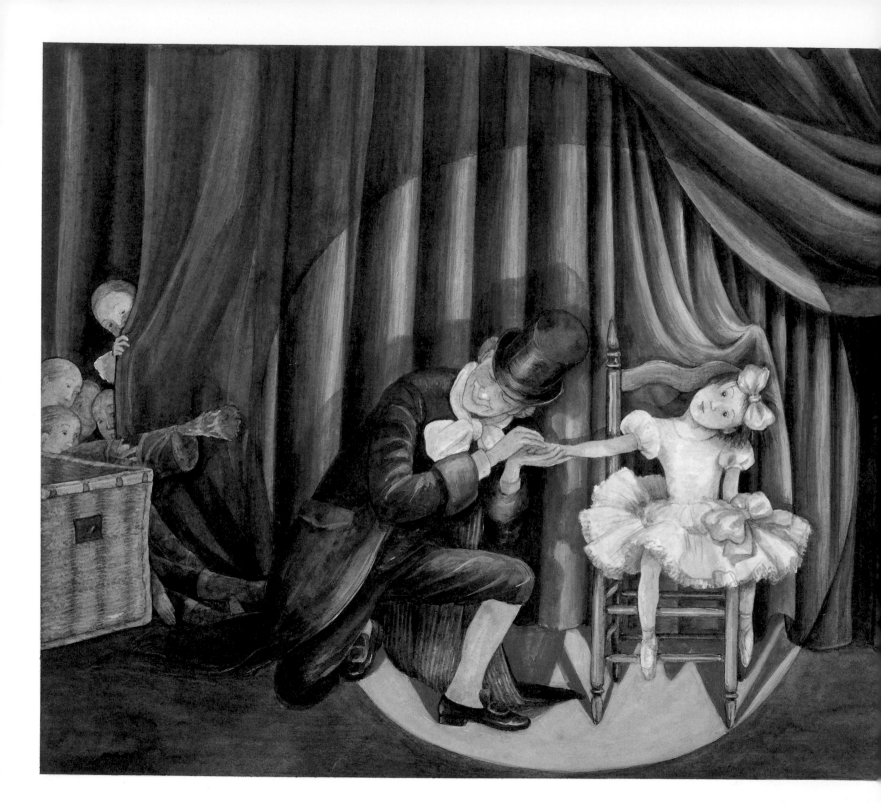

"Until Coppélia grows stiffer and stiffer, and finally stops. She is only a doll, after all. Dr. Coppélius' heart breaks.

"When the village girls run out and tell, the town laughs at the old man. He thought a doll had come to life? Poor fool.

"But, the doctor had a memory of dancing for those few moments with his Coppélia. Dancing around and around, every dance in the world. And that was more precious than gold."

Tanya and the woman bowed to a quiet,
empty room, the door of the old, green
wardrobe still open. "That's why you and
I like tutus, and costumes of every sort,"
the woman, her shoulder more stooped
again, whispered. She hung up the top hat
and the scarf.

There was the shhhh of many voices.

"And here you are," Tanya's mother said, coming through the doorway. "Lost again."

"But I knew where I was," said Tanya, who always did.

"Who were you with?" her mother asked, as they left the room.

"A dancer," Tanya said, turning. The old woman was just a spot of light going down the hall, her arms full of tutus.

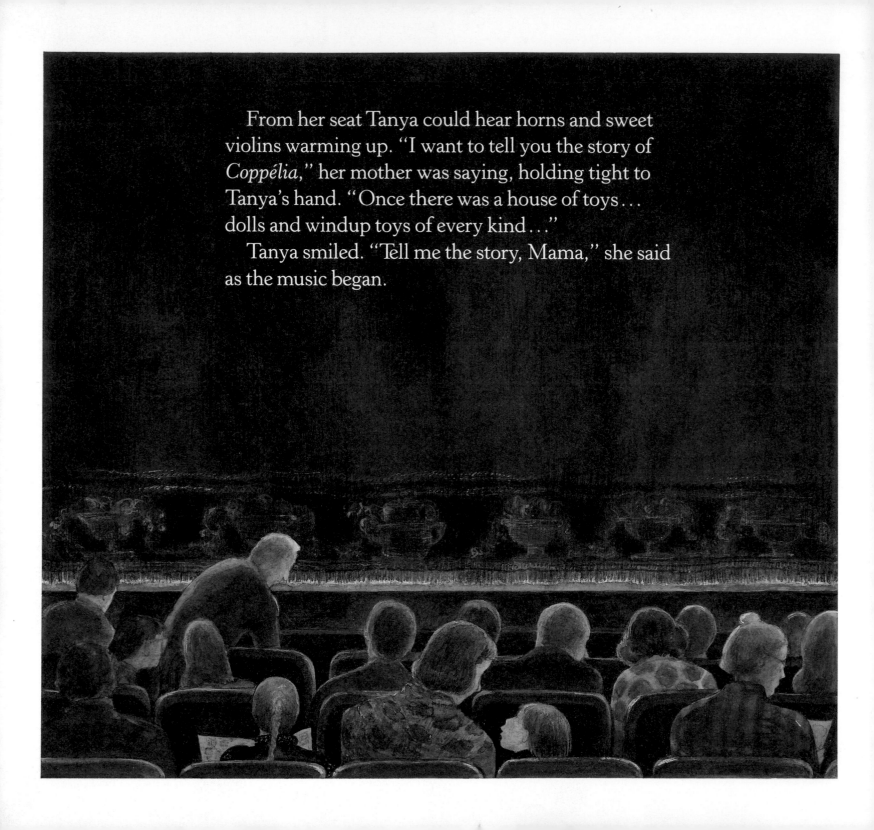

From her seat Tanya could hear horns and sweet violins warming up. "I want to tell you the story of *Coppélia*," her mother was saying, holding tight to Tanya's hand. "Once there was a house of toys... dolls and windup toys of every kind..."

Tanya smiled. "Tell me the story, Mama," she said as the music began.